Written by Jane West

Illustrated by Lee Wildish

FULL FLIGHT

Titles in Full Flight 4

Badger Publishing Limited
15 Wedgwood Gate, Pin Green Industrial Estate,
Stevenage, Hertfordshire SG1 4SU
Telephone: 01438 356907. Fax: 01438 747015
www.badger-publishing.co.uk
enquiries@badger-publishing.co.uk

Striking Out ISBN 1 84691 032 2
　　　　　　ISBN 978-1-84691-032-6

Series Editor: Jonny Zucker
Publisher: David Jamieson
Commissioning Editor: Carrie Lewis
Editor: Paul Martin
Design: Fiona Grant
Illustration: Lee Wildish

Striking Out

Contents

New School

In September, Tess would be going to a new school. Again.

Tess was used to her dad changing jobs. Along with the new job came a new house, new friends and a new school. Tess had been to five new schools. Everyone said it would be easier next time – it never was.

The first day of term wasn't too bad because two girls had been chosen to look after her.

"Hi! I'm Mandy," said the one with glasses.

"And I'm Vaz," said the one with the long, dark hair.

They smiled at her and Tess began to relax. "I'm Teresa," she said shyly, "but everyone calls me 'Tess'."

The new school was pretty okay, but on Wednesday, everything started to go wrong. Tess met Vaz and Mandy for lunch. She got her tray and chose a pizza and salad with a milkshake, and sat down at one of the long tables.

"That's MY seat, maggot," said a hard voice.

Staring down at her was a tall girl with brown hair in a tight ponytail.

"I'm sorry," said Tess quietly. "I didn't know."

"Well, now you do," said the girl, "so move it or lose it."

Tess got up quickly but not before the girl tipped Tess's milkshake all over her pizza.

"Oops!" said the girl, smiling nastily. "Ugh! Looks like baby sick. The maggot is eating baby sick!" and the other girls laughed like drains.

Tess walked quickly away, tears hot in her eyes. She sat down at the back of the room and stared at her soggy lunch.

Vaz and Mandy joined her.

"That was Ellie Jones," said Vaz. "She's a right cow."

"Yes," agreed Mandy, "I've even seen her fight boys – she's a …"

"Everything all right here?" asked a teacher, looking at the three girls.

"Yes," said Tess quietly. "It's fine."

Tess was walking home from school
with Vaz when a voice said, "Oh look!
It's the maggot." Ellie Jones pushed
her large face into Tess's and spat at
her.

Angry and upset Tess yelled, "What
did you do that for?"

"Because I don't like you, maggot,"
hissed Ellie. "What are you looking
at?" she shouted at Vaz.

"Nothing," mumbled Vaz.

"Well, get lost!"

Vaz walked away and Tess was left alone with Ellie Jones and her gang. Ellie lowered her voice as she pushed Tess up against the school fence. "Don't mess with me, maggot, or you'll be sorry. I want five pounds by tomorrow. Same time, same place. Don't tell *anyone*… or else."

She pushed Tess to the ground and kicked her school bag into the gutter, leaving Tess to think what would happen if she did not do as Ellie said.

Tess cried all the way home.

Her mum knew straight away that something was wrong. "What's happened?" she asked.

Tess told her the whole story.

"She sounds like a nasty piece of work," said her mum. "You have to stand up to bullies – they're just cowards – they need a gang to make them feel big. Even so, I want you to tell your form teacher tomorrow."

"But Ellie said I'd be sorry if I did!"

"Bullies can only hurt people if nobody says anything – you have to tell," said her mum gently.

So the next day, Tess told her teacher, Mrs Price.

Telling Lies

Mrs Price said, "Leave it with me."
Just before lunch, Tess was called into
the deputy's office. Ellie was there, too,
in tears.

"I want to hear exactly what's been
going on," said Mr Hill.

Ellie said she'd stopped to chat to Tess
and the bag had fallen into the road
by mistake.

"No!" gasped Tess. "It wasn't like that!
She did it on purpose!"

"Well, I've only got one person's word
against the other, but I'm sure Ellie
would like to apologise for what
happened," said Mr Hill.

"Sorry!" snivelled Ellie.

Ellie's tears stopped the instant they left the office. "You're the one who'll be sorry," she said angrily. "Sorry you ever showed your ugly face in this school… but it will be a lot uglier by the time I've finished with you. See you after school, maggot."

Shakily, Tess walked to the lunch hall. She was about to join Mandy and Vaz when her mobile phone beeped to say she'd got a text message.

It read:

C u after school.

There was no name but Tess knew who'd sent it.

Tess felt like she was going to be sick. She ran to the girls' toilets and hid there until lessons started. Then she slipped out the back and spent the afternoon at the shopping mall until it was time to go home.

Over and over, the same question swam round her head, "What am I going to do?"

"Has that girl bothered you again?" said her mum, kindly.

"No," muttered Tess.

Her mum sighed. "Well, see if there's anything on at the local cinema. We could go tonight and cheer you up."

Tess flicked through the local paper looking for the cinema page but her eye was caught by an advert.

**SELF-DEFENCE COURSE
FOR BEGINNERS**

**Learn Judo and
discover a new you!**

**6.30pm Tuesday
at Hamble Town Hall**

"That's it!" said Tess excitedly. "That's just what I need!" Tess asked her mum if it was okay for her to go.

"I think it is a brilliant idea," said Tess's mum.

The town hall was full of people in white judo suits and a small group of people like Tess in T-shirts and tracksuit bottoms.

"Welcome!" said a young woman. "My name is Jen and I'm going to teach you how to defend yourselves."

Jen was small and slim and not much taller than Tess.

"I'll show you that size doesn't matter."

A huge, hulking man with tattoos on his bulging muscles stood next to her.

"Neil is going to *try* to throw me," said Jen.

Neil lunged at Jen, but she darted out of the way, grabbed the front of his shirt and threw him over her shoulder. He landed with a thud on the floor.

"Wow!" said Tess. "That was so cool!"

"Thanks," said Jen, "but you'll be able to do that soon!"

Tess spent the next hour learning some simple self-defence moves and she went home hot, sweaty and tired, but happy.

"Just you wait, Ellie Jones," she said to herself. "Just you wait!"

Waiting...

Tess went to self-defence classes for the next four weeks. She enjoyed it so much that she talked her mum into letting her join the judo training, too.

She felt pretty cool in her judo suit, although it was annoying having to keep her nails so short.
She learned how to fall without hurting herself and how to throw people off balance who were heavier and taller than she was.

Jen had been right about that – size didn't matter when you knew judo.

At school, Tess kept out of Ellie's way, although she sometimes saw Ellie watching her from a distance.

The text messages kept coming, but even though Tess didn't read them, she didn't delete them. She knew the day was coming when Ellie would have another go at her – this time Tess would be ready AND she'd got proof that Ellie was a bully. But the text messages really got on her nerves.

One day, Tess, Vaz and Mandy were sitting in their form room when Tess got another text from Ellie. It said:

2nite, maggot. Nowhere 2 hide. No 1 will help u.

Mandy and Vaz looked sacred but Tess said, "Ellie Jones is a big, fat cow, but she doesn't scare me."

They looked at her in shock, but Tess carried on unpacking her bag, smiling to herself.

Sweet Revenge!

That lunchtime, Tess was standing in the food queue when Ellie Jones came up to her. "I'm gonna get you tonight," she hissed.

"Do I look bothered?" said Tess in a bored voice.

"Move, maggot!" shouted Ellie and she went to push Tess.

In a flash, Tess grabbed at the arm that was pushing her, span on the spot like she'd been taught in judo and pulled hard. Ellie skidded on the floor and landed face first in the pizza with her skirt over her head and her big, white, granny knickers on display to the whole school.

The carton of milkshake exploded like a bomb, covering Ellie's head with strawberry-flavoured goo.

Mandy and Vaz started giggling and Tess laughed out loud – soon the whole lunchroom was shrieking with laughter as Ellie tried to sort out her skirt with pizza sauce dripping down her nose.

"You've spoiled my lunch, pizza face!" laughed Tess.

"Miss Jones!" said the lunchtime supervisor. "I won't have bullying in my lunchroom – you'll be excluded this time!"

Ellie was marched off to the deputy's office, her face burning with shame and pink milkshake dripping down her hair and onto her pizza-covered face, leaving a slimy trail behind her.

"That was amazing!" shouted Vaz.

"I can teach you, if you like," said Tess, smiling. "But I don't think Ellie Jones will be bullying anyone ever again... not if she knows what's good for her!"